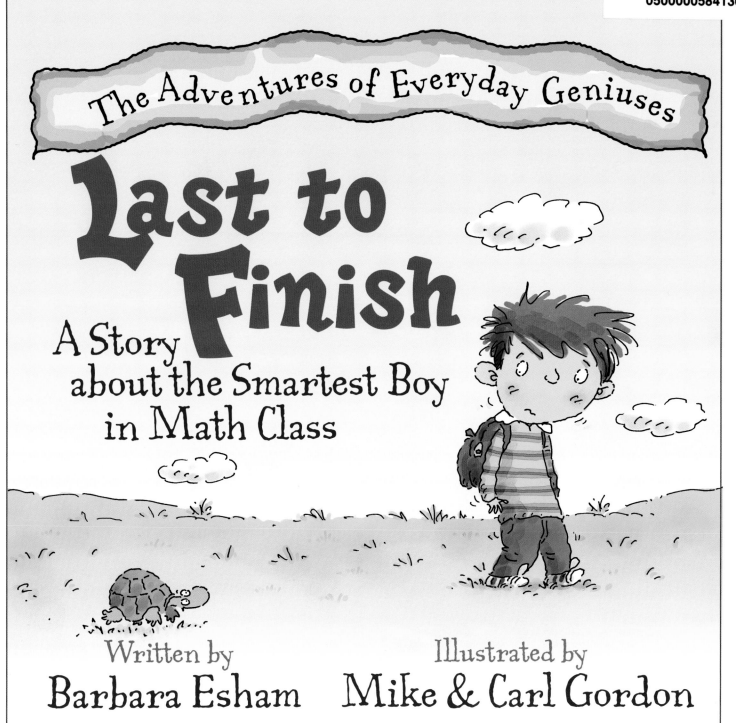

The Adventures of Everyday Geniuses

Last to Finish

A Story about the Smartest Boy in Math Class

Written by
Barbara Esham

Illustrated by
Mike & Carl Gordon

Published by Mainstream Connections, Perry Hall, MD
ISBN 978-1-60336-456-0 • LCCN 2007908045

I always thought that math was going to be my thing.
My dad is an engineer, and he always says that
math is the key to success.

It is just my luck that the door to success is
locked with the "math" keys.

I'm Max Leonhard, and I'm a third grader at
Perryville Elementary School.
This year has been a bit tough for me because
it's the first time that I ever
felt I was terrible at something...

2

...and that doesn't feel so good.

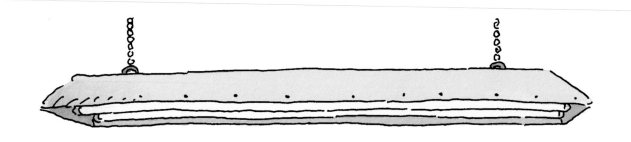

The problem started when Mrs. Topel, our teacher, started using the timer to test us on our multiplication facts. If I take my time, I can get every one of my math facts without any problem at all!

4

The problem comes when I have to finish them in record time –
like a sprinter running toward the finish line,
hoping to break the world record.
The timer works just fine for some kids, like David Peterson.
He likes to be the first to finish everything!

It doesn't work for me.
As soon as Mrs. Topel starts the timer,
my heart begins to pound,
my hands begin to sweat,
and then the worst thing happens...

...my mind freezes.

It happened again today.
One by one, my classmates finished their math facts.
I knew the answers last night when I did my practice test,
but they disappeared today!

All I could think about was that terrible timer
ticking that terrible tick-tick-tick!

What happened? Are math facts erased from my mind while I sleep? Why does 2x3 suddenly look like an alien message that can only be deciphered by scientists?

"Time is up,"
Mrs. Topel announced.

I was the last one to hand in my paper and I still had twenty problems to go. Just when I thought things couldn't get any worse, David Peterson whispered, "Max, Max, last in math."

In the lunch room after math,
David continued to tease me.

Why does David Peterson have to be so cruel?
Does embarrassing me make David Peterson feel important?

The chanting started up again during recess, like I knew it would.

The chanting was so loud, even the preschool class heard it.
They thought it was okay to chant along.

"Max, Max, last in math!"

After school, I went straight home to do my homework,
and the day got even worse. I couldn't find my math folder.

I emptied my backpack to search for it,
which wasn't such a bad idea...
I needed to get rid of a few things.

"Mom, I can't find my math folder," I admitted.
It was embarrassing.

"Max, you are going to have to be more responsible with your school work, especially your math materials," she replied.

Sometimes I get the feeling that my mom and dad are disappointed in me. I know they love me, but I want them to be proud of me too.

Maybe I'm just disappointed in myself.

Timed math facts have ruined everything!

16

"Max, Mrs. Topel and Mr. Singleton have asked us to attend a meeting. They want to discuss your math performance.

I'm sure that everything will be just fine. Remember, Max, your dad and I are proud of your hard work. You may just need to work a little harder," my mom said with a smile.

My parents had been encouraging about the conference,
but I was nervous when it was time to meet a few days later.
I expected Mrs. Topel and Mr. Singleton to tell Mom and Dad
that I was the worst math student they'd ever taught at
Perryville Elementary.

The fateful day arrived.

"Mr. and Mrs. Leonhard, thank you for taking the time to meet with us today," Mr. Singleton said with a serious voice.

"About two weeks ago, I found Max's math folder in the hallway. I didn't return it because I was very surprised by the math exercises Max has been working on," he added.

"We thought it was important that we discuss Max's math ability with you," Mrs. Topel said.

Math ability? I thought... What math ability? I'm always the last to finish my math facts. I guess it's the **lack** of ability we'll be talking about. I knew this conference wouldn't be good...

"How long has Max been practicing algebra I?"
Mr. Singleton asked.

"Algebra I? There must be a mistake," my dad said.
"Max is only in third grade." My mom looked confused.
"Max, what is Mr. Singleton talking about?"

"Algebra is something I do for fun. It's like a puzzle.
I finished my older brother's pre-algebra book last year,
so sometimes I borrow his algebra I book —
if he isn't using it of course," I said quietly.

"All this time, we've been concerned about Max's
math performance. He has struggled with memorizing
multiplication facts all year," my dad said.

"Max has been asked to memorize math facts. That is difficult for some children and adults," Mr. Singleton explained. Max is the type of math student who understands how numbers work together. He may not be the type of student who learns by memorization. Some people are great at memorizing all sorts of information, while others are great at understanding information. If I could choose between the two, I would rather have students understand mathematics," Mr. Singleton said with a smile. "You need your thinking cap for algebra, and Max seems to be wearing his a bit early."

"Does this mean that Max will move ahead to algebra?"
my dad asked with pride.

"We will need to be sure that Max has a complete understanding of the math concepts leading up to algebra. Max will work
in a program for accelerated math students, so he can build on
what he has mastered," said Mr. Singleton. "I would also like
him to join our math team. He would make a fine addition."

"Me? On the math team?
That is the strangest thing I have ever heard!" I said.

"Not really, Max. You seem to be an algebra whiz.
Let's give it a try," my dad added, quite proudly.

"Well, maybe I'll give it a try, but under one condition..."

"No timer!"

From Dr. Edward Hallowell,

New York Times national best seller, former Harvard Medical School instructor, and current director of the Hallowell Center for Cognitive and Emotional Health...

Fear is the great disabler. Fear is what keeps children from realizing their potential. It needs to be replaced with a feeling of I-know-I-can-make-progress-if-I-keep-trying-and-boy-do-I-ever-want-to-do-that!

One of the great goals of parents, teachers, and coaches should be to find areas in which a child might experience mastery, then make it possible for the child to feel this potent sensation.

The feeling of mastery transforms a child from a reluctant, fearful learner into a self-motivated player.

The mistake that parents, teachers, and coaches often make is that they demand mastery rather than lead children to it by helping them overcome the fear of failure.

The best parents are great teachers. My definition of a great teacher is a person who can lead another person to mastery.

~Dr. Hallowell

To read Dr. Hallowell's full letter, go to our website! Check out what ALL THE OTHER EXPERTS are saying about The Adventures of Everyday Geniuses book series. www.MainstreamConnections.org

A Note to Parents & Teachers

Mainstream Connections would like to help you help your kids become **Everyday Geniuses!**

These fun stories are an easy way to discuss learning styles and obstacles that can impede a child's potential.

The science of learning is making its way into the classroom! Everyday Geniuses are making their debut!

Call, email, or visit the website to learn how YOU can make a difference.

All books are available in bulk at discount for qualifying schools and professional organizations. Contact us!

The Adventures of Everyday Geniuses

RESOURCES for PARENTS and TEACHERS

The BIG LIST of resources can be found on our website. The big list is for parents and teachers, you know, just to give them the latest information on how our brains really learn, and what being smart is all about.

The topics of this book – MATH FACTS and MEMORIZATION – are learning obstacles for many Everyday Geniuses. Rote math skills have little to do with potential aptitude for more advanced math. Albert Einstein would have agreed...

Mainstream Connections provides you respected resources to help you create a happy, healthy learning environment for every child.

DOWNLOAD your complimentary Resource List today!

WEBSITES
Links to great sites to learn more about learning styles.

BOOK LISTS
Learn what the experts say about learning styles and obstacles.

CONNECT
News, info & support!

www.MainstreamConnections.org

The Mainstream Connections mission is to expose the broader definitions of learning, creativity, and intelligence. A substantial portion of all profits is held to fund and support the development of programs and services to give all children the tools needed for success.

Are you an EVERYDAY GENIUS TOO?

Get online with your favorite characters from

The Adventures of Everyday Geniuses

There is SO MUCH to do online!

- Meet the Gang and see what they are up to: ideas, inventions and algorithms, poems and other literary works, sEduardo's latest recipe, and get a list of great minds from the past and present!
- Download pages for coloring!
- Hats, Shirts, Classroom Stuff!

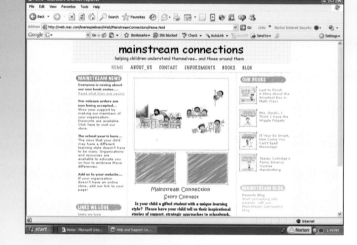

www.MainstreamConnections.org

Visit our website to learn more! Adults should always supervise children's web activity.

BOOK INFORMATION

Last To Finish: A Story about the Smartest Boy in Math Class
written by Barbara Esham illustrated by Mike & Carl Gordon

Published by Mainstream Connections Publishing
P.O. Box 398, Perry Hall Maryland 21128

Copyright © 2008, Barbara Esham. All rights reserved.

No part of this publication may be reproduced in whole or in part, in any form without permission from the publisher. *The Adventures of Everyday Geniuses* is a registered trademark.

Book design by Pneuma Books, LLC. www.pneumabooks.com

Printed in China ∞ Library Binding

FIRST EDITION

15 14 13 12 11 10 09 08   01 02 03 04 05 06 07 08

CATALOGING-IN-PUBLICATION DATA

Esham, Barbara.

Last to finish : a story about the smartest boy in math class / written by Barbara Esham ; illustrated by Mike & Carl Gordon. -- 1st ed. -- Perry Hall, MD : Mainstream Connections, 2008.

p. ; cm.

(Adventures of everyday geniuses)

ISBN: 978-1-60336-456-0

Audience: Ages 5-10.

Summary: Max Leonard is convinced that he will never succeed with memorizing his multiplication tables; and his brain "freezes"during timed tests. But to everyone's surprise, Max has been completing algebra problem sets in his spare time! Max, his parents and teachers are amazed by his math "potential".

1. Mathematical ability in children--Juvenile fiction. 2. Math anxiety--Juvenile fiction. 3. Self-esteem--Juvenile fiction. 4. Learning disabled children--Juvenile fiction. 5. Cognitive styles in children. 6. [Mathematical ability--Fiction. 7. Math anxiety. 8. Learning disabilities--Fiction.] I. Gordon, Mike. II. Gordon, Carl. III. Title. IV. Series.

PZ7.E74583 L37 2008   2007908045

[Fic]--dc22   0804